DEDICATION

He who buys this book may make

the dedication to the child who receives it

First Chronicle Books edition published in 2005.

Copyright © 1963 by Bruno Munari.
Originally published in the United States in 1963 by The World Publishing Company.
All rights reserved by Maurizio Corraini srl – Italy.

ISBN 978-0-8118-4830-5
Manufactured in Italy, July 2009.

Library of Congress Cataloging-in-Publication Data available.

10 9 8 7 6 5 4 3

This product conforms to CPSIA 2008.

Chronicle Books LLC
680 Second Street, San Francisco, California 94107

www.chroniclekids.com

Bruno Munari's

ZOO

NOTICE

Don't feed the animals: don't give the birds to the fox, the fox to the lion, the parrot to the tiger. Don't annoy the butterflies. Leave the signs where they are. The lion will be offended if you pull his tail. It is forbidden to sit on the tortoise or to play with the bears. Applaud the seals.

BIRDS

SEALS

FEROCIOUS ANIMALS

FLAMINGOS
SNAKES
ZEBRAS
PARROT
SQUIRREL
FOX
HIPPOPOTAMUS
CAMEL
PORCUPINE

The parrot was born on a day with rainbow.

When it rains, birds seek shelter under the elephant.

Flamingos know
they are beautiful
and strange,
and play at symmetry.

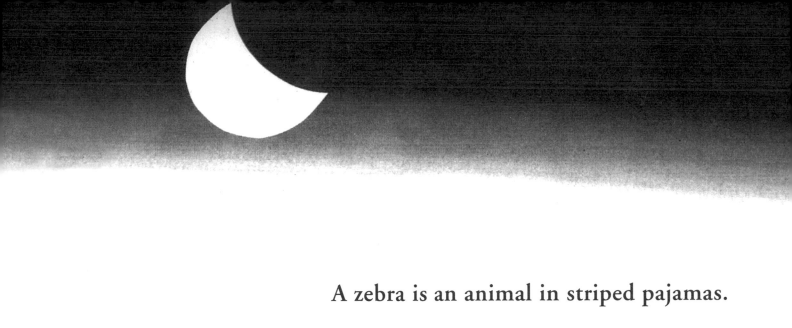

A zebra is an animal in striped pajamas.

The lion
does not fear
anyone.

The squirrel
spends the summer
storing nuts
for the winter.

A rhinoceros is always ready to fight.

The snake knots and unknots itself.

The fox hides when he sees the furrier.

The birds are infinite.

Some camels are more humpy than others. This one has a seat for you.

Seals like a circus every day.

Monkeys use their hands
as feet
and their feet
as hands.

A tiger is a big cat with stripes.

A leopard is a big cat with spots.

For the hippopotamus
the swimming pool is always too small.

The peacock stalks proudly because he is the peacock.

A kangaroo is all legs, but he does not know it.

If bears played baseball,
polar bears would be umpires.

The porcupine loses himself among the grasses.

Tortoises are as old as the mountains.